This book is dedicated to Mrs. Johnson.

Have you ever been sat on
Nearly every single day?
Or bent, twisted or ridden on
In so many incorrect ways?

Can you imagine someone standing on you
Or jumping on your seat,
Pounding on your body
With their yucky, stinky feet?

Of course you haven't, why would you?
This is not a normal thing,
To be mistreated and misused
As if you were a swing.

Children look at us at parks and playgrounds and think,
"Oh, I'd like to swing on that."
But they're never just carefully swinging,
They're usually tossing us front and back.

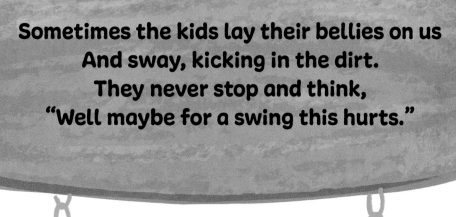

Sometimes the kids lay their bellies on us
And sway, kicking in the dirt.
They never stop and think,
"Well maybe for a swing this hurts."

Sometimes, they ride us backwards,
Twist our chains up in a knot.
We're more sensitive than children
Or their parents ever thought!

It's bad enough we're stuck outside
In rain, sleet, and snow,
Or that we're left alone
After the families all up and go.

But even when they're with us,
People mistreat us, the playground swings.
Does anyone seem to care?
No! All that matters is the joy we bring.

Well, one day, we had enough
Of being treated badly everyday.
We wanted to take a stand
And knew that going on strike was the only way!

So we unclipped our seats and took our chains,
We hid behind the picnic bench.
We wrote the children a letter
To explain why we were so tense.

"Dear children, we've had enough!
You cannot treat us however you'd like.
We're tired of you standing on us and riding us the wrong way.
We've decided to go on STRIKE!

You lay down on your bellies and kick off,
Launching at the sky.
Did you ever stop to think
We do NOT like going too, too high?

You swing and swing and swing
And then jump off suddenly to the ground.
It surprises us and jerks us,
It's a bad feeling all around.

You twist around our chains
And then let go to spin and spin.
We get dizzy as we worry
You'll fall off and scrape your chin.

We left the note below the swing set
And the kids found it right away.
They searched the playground until they found us
And they had something to say:

When we do those things,
We're just trying to have fun with you,
But we understand if leaning back or jumping off
Are things we shouldn't do."

When we heard how much joy we gave the kids,
We decided to say OK,
As long as they didn't sit on us wrong
Every single day.

And from then on, as they swung on us,
The kids' smiles seemed extra wide.
Maybe they just needed to see things
From their friends, the swings', side!

Made in United States
Orlando, FL
02 August 2022

20479300R00022